Disney Cuties
Doodle Book

DISNEY PRESS
New York

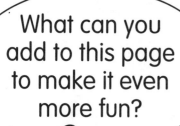

What can you add to this page to make it even more fun?

Printed in the United States of America

First Edition

10 9 8 7 6 5 4 3 2 1

V381-8386-5-11060

ISBN 978-1-4231-4054-2

For more Disney Press fun, visit www.disneybooks.com

DISNEP PRESS
New York

It's a great day for planting a garden. Help Mickey and Minnie fill in the flower bed.

Oh, no! Donald's car is leaving without him. Draw another way for him to get where he's going.

Trace the names of the characters below their pictures.

Mickey

Minnie

Chip

Dale

Goofy

Pluto

Donald

Daisy

Daisy and Minnie are busy baking delicious treats. Draw a plate of goodies for Daisy. What else do they need in the kitchen?

Flower sure loves flowers! Make his flower bed even prettier by coloring three flowers red, two flowers yellow, and five flowers purple. Make all the stems and leaves green.

Goofy is learning addition. Help him solve the puzzles on the blackboard!

Aa Bb C

Pluto has chased something up a tree, but what? Draw an animal high up in the branches. What else could Pluto chase?

Daisy loves the beach! Draw an umbrella to help her stay cool. What else does she need for her beach day?

Mickey and Minnie are looking up
at the stars. Connect the dots from
1 to 25 to find the constellation.

Dale sent Chip a secret message about where his acorns are hidden. Help him decode it, then circle the hiding place.

Jkgx Inov,

Znk giuxty gxk

nojjkt ot znk

znoxj zxkk lxus

znk rklz.

Jgrk

DEAR CHIP,

THE ACORNS ARE

HIDDEN IN THE

THIRD TREE FROM

THE LEFT.

DALE

GHIJKLMNOPQRSTUVWXYZABCDEF
ABCDEFGHIJKLMNOPQRSTUVWXYZ

Mickey and Goofy are spending the day fishing.
Draw what they've caught so far on the shore.
What else is in the water?

Oops! Bambi slipped on the ice! Give him some friends to teach him how to skate!

Read the description of each character.
Then circle the one who fits it best.

I live in the forest. My best friends are a rabbit and a skunk.

Mickey is my best friend! We love to go on walks together.

Gawrsh! I love hanging out with Mickey and Donald!

My favorite food is nuts! I love to steal them from Donald!

Something's not right in this scene. Can you find five things that are out of place?

Minnie's shopping for a new outfit, but this one isn't quite right. Draw some new shirts for her to try on. What else might she buy?

Donald is helping Daisy in her garden.
He has three baskets of carrots and three
baskets of apples. Can you help him find them?

Pluto loves going for a walk! Fill in the things that he and Mickey pass.

There are six differences between these two scenes. Can you find them all?

How many times does each Donald appear?
Count them up and then put the number next
to the right pose.

= 5

= 4

= 6

Chip and Dale hid their acorns, and now they can't find them. Can you find 12 acorns?

Help Minnie get to the table Daisy saved.

Mickey, Donald, and Goofy are racing sailboats down the river. Add two more boats to the scene and give the winner a prize!

Match the Cuties to their shadows by drawing lines between them.

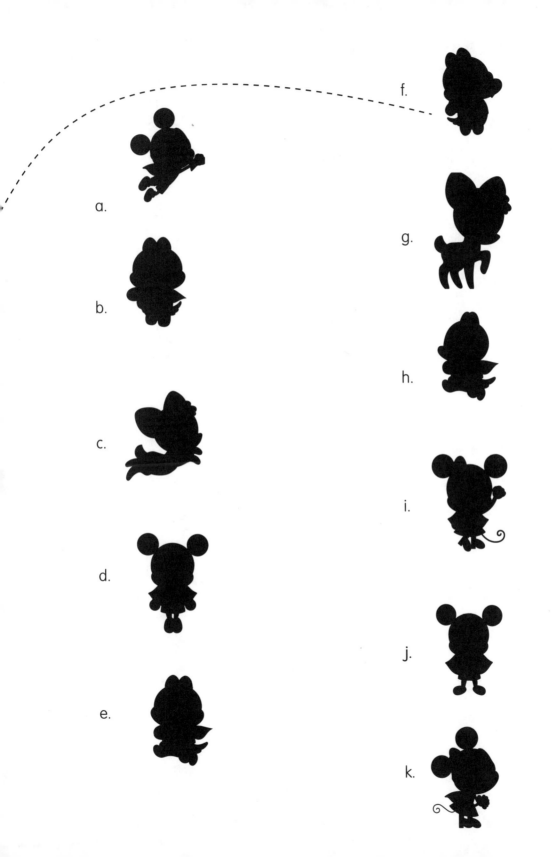

a.

b.

c.

d.

e.

f.

g.

h.

i.

j.

k.

Thumper's name appears in the grid 10 times. Can you find all 10? They may run across, down, or backward. Cross his name off the list each time you find it in the grid.

1. THUMPER   6. THUMPER

2. THUMPER   7. THUMPER

3. THUMPER   8. THUMPER

4. THUMPER   9. THUMPER

5. THUMPER   10. THUMPER

T	T	H	T	T	H	U	M	P	E	R
H	U	M	H	P	E	R	T	H	U
U	T	H	U	M	P	E	R	P	R
M	H	E	M	R	T	H	E	U	E
P	U	U	P	H	T	R	P	E	P
E	M	M	E	T	H	U	M	E	M
R	P	P	R	E	R	T	U	H	U
P	E	R	E	P	M	U	H	T	H
E	R	E	P	M	U	H	T	R	T
T	H	U	M	P	E	R	M	U	H

Pluto is trying to find his way to Mickey. Which line will lead him there?

Mmmm . . . Minnie sure is having fun at the carnival! What foods do you like to eat at a carnival? Draw more food stands and some rides for Minnie to enjoy.

Donald and Daisy are looking out at the river together. What do they see? What else is happening in this scene?

SuperMickey has saved Minnie! Add what he saved her from to the scene. Who else can SuperMickey save?

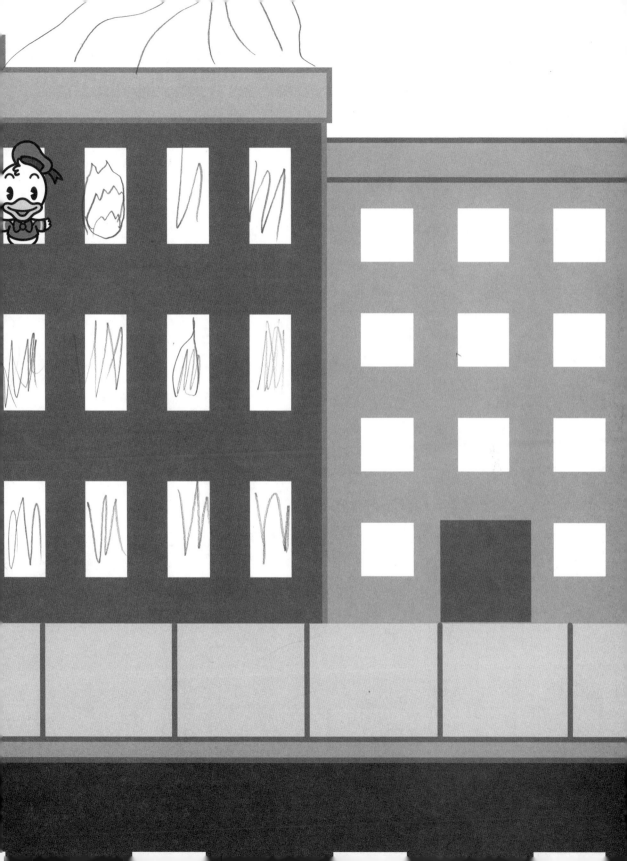

It's Mickey's birthday! Solve the equations and then color each section according to the code in the table below.

Balloons $3 + 4 =$ __7__

Banner $5 + 1 =$ __6__

Cake $3 + 6 =$ __9__

Goofy's hat $5 + 2 =$ __7__

Mickey's pants $1 + 4 =$ __5__

Donald's hat $3 + 3 =$ __6__

Pluto $6 + 2 =$ __8__

Minnie's hat $4 + 5 =$ __9__

Tablecloth $3 + 7 =$ __10__

Presents $2 + 3 =$ __5__

Code:					
5	6	7	8	9	10
Red	Blue	Green	Orange	Pink	Yellow

Chip and Dale are having a party.
Give Chip a stick and a pinata to hit.

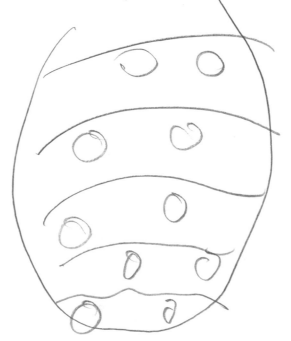

Minnie and Daisy are having a sleepover. Help decorate the room for the party.

What are Mickey and his friends celebrating?
Draw a picture of it.

All of Bambi's friends are resting for the winter.
Give him some new friends to play with.

Study the scene below carefully. Then turn the page to answer questions about it.

1. **How many clouds are there in the sky?**

   3

2. **What color is Daisy's bucket?**

   Pink

3. **What color is Donald's shovel?**

   Green

4. **How many rays does the sun have?**

   Eight

5. Who is going for a swim?

Goofy

6. What are Donald and Daisy building?

Sand castle

7. How many stripes are there on the towel?

11

8. What color are Daisy's shoes?

PURPLE

What has Goofy so surprised?
Draw a picture of it.

Chip and Dale are great friends! Draw a picture of your best friend.

What's happening in each panel? Fill in Mickey and Minnie's day with your own story.

Pluto wants to see what's going on outside! Draw an outdoors scene for him to look at!

Something's not right in this scene. Can you find five things that are out of place?

What is Thumper laughing at?
Draw it in the box.

Chip and Dale have made a mess again, and Donald is furious! Draw in their mess. What do you think Donald is saying to them?

**Mickey and his friends love snowy days.
There's so much to do!**

Mickey and Donald go ice-skating on the frozen pond.

Goofy is sledding. "Come on, Mickey!" he cries. "First one to the bottom wins!"

Donald's at the bottom of the hill making a snowduck. What fun!

How about snow *angels*?

Uh-oh. Mickey's making snowballs.
Watch out, Goofy and Donald!

Smack! Mickey's snowballs hit Goofy and Donald right in the head!

Time to go inside and warm up.
Hot cocoa for everyone . . . *Mmmm!*

Yum! **Minnie and Daisy love to eat ice cream! What's your favorite kind of ice cream? Draw a big cone for yourself in the box.**

Bambi is lost and can't find his way home. Turn the meadow into a forest and give him a path to follow.

Oh, no! Poor Minnie got stuck in the rain! Give her an umbrella to stay dry. Then draw some rainy-day activities for her in the thought bubble.

Mickey's had a long day, and he needs a rest! What is he dreaming about?

Donald's feeling creative today!
Help him paint a picture of Daisy.

Mickey and his friends are marching in a parade. Give them flags to hold and instruments to play.

Mickey, Donald, and Goofy had their pictures taken and hung them on the wall. Draw pictures of their other friends in the empty frames.

Mickey and Minnie are off to the movies for the night. Draw a picture of what they're seeing in the box.

This picture of Bambi and Thumper is all mixed up. Label the correct spot for each piece.

 and are spending the day together.

"Let's work on your ," said .

"No. Let's go for ," said .

"Why don't we read a ," said .

But still said no. She wanted !

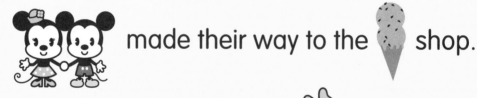 made their way to the shop.

On the way there, they passed . She was on

her way to meet .

"You and  should join us for ,"

 said.

Soon all four were on their way.

When  opened the door to the

shop, he saw all of his friends inside.

"Surprise!"  shouted.

There were 🎁🎁 everywhere. It was a party

for  ! No wonder  wanted  !

Daisy's making an important phone call. Draw who she's talking to in the thought bubble.

Answer the questions about the scene below to solve the crossword puzzle.

Across

1: What color is the grass?

4: What color are the ducks?

5: What color are Mickey's pants?

Down

1: Who is standing next to Mickey?

2: What are there two of in the sky?

3: How many ducks are in the water?

SuperMickey is taking flight! What superpower would you like to have? Draw a picture of yourself with the power.

Zooooooooooom!!!

Mickey, Donald, and Goofy are building a snow fort! Help them build it up. Then give them some snowballs to defend the fort.

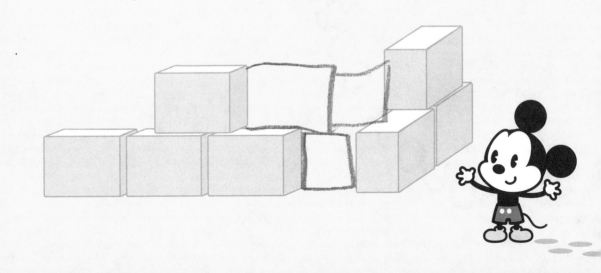

Fizzz... Chef Minnie made herself an awesome ice cream soda! What's your favorite summertime drink? Draw a picture of it. What else do you like to eat in the summer?

Which Mickey isn't the same? Circle him. Then draw your own Mickey that is different from the others.

Donald opened a lemonade stand, but no one's buying anything! Give him a better sign and some customers.

Bambi and Thumper are looking for their friend Flower. Add him to the scene. Who else do they find?

Mickey sent Goofy a secret message about what he wants to do this weekend. Help him decode it, then circle the object Goofy will need to bring with him.

Uvri Xffwp,
Cvk'j xf wzjyzex
kyzj nvvbveu!
Pfli wizveu,
Dztbvp

D _ _ _   _ _ _ _ _ _,

_ _ _ _   _ _   _ _ _ _ _ _ _

_ _ _ _   _ _ _ _ _ _ _!

_ _ _ _   _ _ _ _ _ _,

_ _ _ _ _ _

R S T U V W X Y Z A B C D E F G H I J K L M N O P Q
A B C D E F G H I J K L M N O P Q R S T U V W X Y Z

Minnie and Daisy are having a tea party. Draw a teapot and teacups for them. What else do they need?

Mickey and Pluto are throwing a party! Help them decorate the room!

Chip and Dale are making a comic. Fill in the boxes with your own drawings.

1. Chip and Dale are hungry. Where can they find something to eat?

2. Chip has an idea.

3. Donald always has the best food!

4. Uh-oh, looks like Donald's angry again!

Mickey and Donald are playing a game of volleyball. Draw a net between them. What else might they bring to the beach?

Find the picture that only appears once and circle it.

Goofy brought an apple to school for his teacher. Write his name on the board with a star next to it. Then add his favorite teacher to the scene.

Aa Bb Cc

Chip and Dale are eating all the food in Donald's cabinet. Fill in the shelves with their favorites!

Mickey picked flowers for Minnie. Help him solve these problems to color in the scene.

Flowers	$3 + 4 = \underline{\hspace{2cm}}$
Sun	$7 - 2 = \underline{\hspace{2cm}}$
Grass	$1 + 8 = \underline{\hspace{2cm}}$
Mickey's pants	$9 - 3 = \underline{\hspace{2cm}}$
Mickey's shoes	$1 + 4 = \underline{\hspace{2cm}}$
Sky	$3 + 5 = \underline{\hspace{2cm}}$
Dirt	$9 - 5 = \underline{\hspace{2cm}}$

Code:

4	5	6	7	8	9
Brown	Yellow	Red	Pink	Blue	Green

Minnie loves the rain, but her favorite part of a rainy day is seeing a rainbow. Add a rainbow to the scene to make Minnie's day perfect!

Thumper sure has a big family! Add all of his brothers and sisters to the scene!

Mickey is picking apples for Minnie.
Give him a basket to hold the fruit.
What will he need to reach the apples?

What do each of the characters below want to be when they grow up? Dress them up for different jobs. Draw a picture of what you want to be when you grow up.

Minnie and Daisy are playing hopscotch.
Draw a board for them on the sidewalk.
What else is going on around them?

Mickey and Goofy are building a cabin in the woods. Draw the tools they need to finish the job!

It's Chip and Dale to the rescue! Give the two heroes a bad guy to fight. What else is going on in the scene?

Pretend your friend doesn't know Mickey and his pals. Write two complete sentences to describe each character below.

_____

_____

_____

_____

Mickey and Minnie are flying
kites, but something's missing!
Add the kites to the ends of their
strings. What else is happening
in the park?

There are six differences in these two scenes.
Can you find them all?

Help Chip and Dale reach their acorns.

Mickey and Minnie are going to the petting zoo. Add some fuzzy animals for them to play with.

Gawrsh! Goofy and Mickey were blowing bubbles, but Goofy's exploded all over his face! Draw a new bubble for him. Then give Mickey and Goofy more friends to join in the fun.

POP!

Daisy is ready for bed, but first she needs a bedtime story. Write the beginning of a story for her.

1. What does Goofy have in his mouth?

_____

2. How many raindrops are there?

_____

3. Is Goofy wearing a hat?

_____

4. Who is going for a walk?

_____

5. How many ripples are there in the water around Goofy?

_____

6. How many clouds are there in the sky?

_____

7. How many trees are there?

_____

8. How many stripes are there on Goofy's swimsuit?

_____

Minnie made 10 cupcakes, but she lost them. Can you help her find them?

Pluto loves jumping in leaves. Draw some leaves flying out of the pile. Then give him a friend to play with.

Minnie and Daisy are relaxing on the beach. What else do they need to make their day perfect?

Write the name of each character on the next page. Then find their names in the word search. They may run across or down.

```
Z  W  I  G  O  B  P
Q  A  H  C  P  A  F
R  L  S  K  C  M  M
J  T  I  T  T  B  D
N  L  K  C  H  I  P
V  U  X  A  U  U  M
B  D  Q  G  M  D  H
E  A  J  O  P  Y  N
F  L  O  W  E  R  V
W  E  F  R  R  B  S
```

DALE

CHIP

THUMPER

FLOWER

BAMBI

Minnie loves to ice-skate. Give her skates, a scarf, and a special skating outfit. Then give her a friend to skate with!

Look! Goofy bought you a present!
Draw a picture of what's in the box.

 loves every season, but his favorite

time of year is the spring! The grow

. The  bloom. And best of all,

 gets to see his friends!

One spring day, ,  , and

decided to play hide-and-seek. was it!

 looked everywhere. In the bushes.

Near the stream. Finally he found hiding

in some  .

 and  looked for

together. But he was nowhere to be seen.

Suddenly heard giggling.

It was . He was hiding in a big  .

Found you,  !

**Mickey and Pluto are the best of buddies.
Draw more friends for them to play with.**

Donald and Daisy are shopping together. What do you think they bought? Draw it in the box.

What's happening in each panel? Fill in Mickey, Goofy, and Donald's day with your own story.

Chip and Dale have spent all winter dreaming about nuts. What do you dream about? Draw a picture of it.

Mickey and Goofy have started a book club. What are they reading? Give the book a title and draw a cover for it.

There's simply nothing better than a sale!
Minnie and Daisy have spent all day shopping.
Fill the closet with their new clothes.

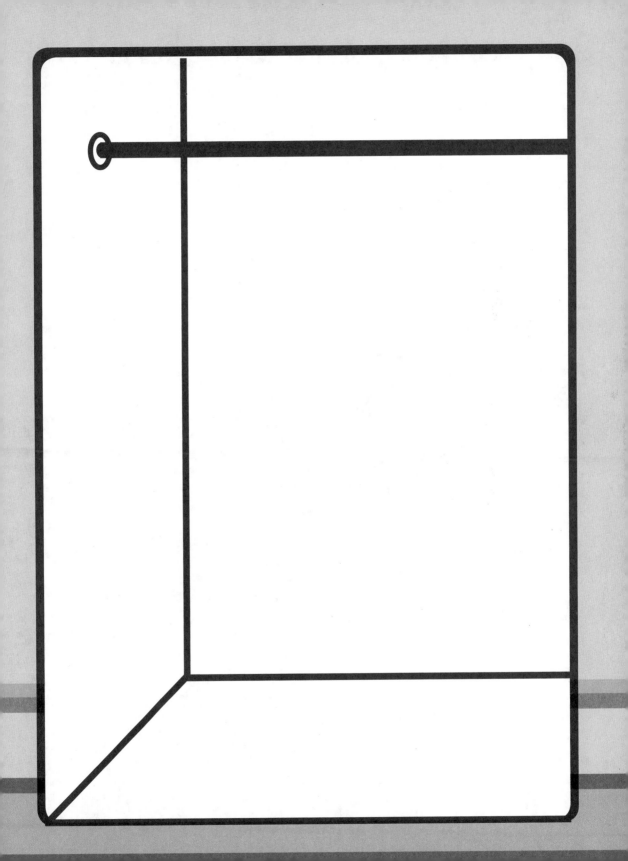

Something's not right in this scene. Can you find six things that are out of place?

Poor Pluto lost his bone. Help him think about where it might be.

Daisy is chilling out with some cold pink lemonade. Draw a special straw for her. What snacks would cool her off? Draw them, too!

Study the scene below carefully. Then turn the page to answer questions about it.

1. How many buildings are in the scene?

_____

2. How many boxes is Mickey carrying?

_____

3. In which direction is the car driving?

_____

4. Which characters are in the windows?

_____

5. What color is the tallest building?

_____

6. What color is Minnie's skirt?

_____

7. How many windows are there?

_____

8. What color box does Mickey only have one of?

_____

9. What is Minnie holding in her hand?

_____

10. How many squares are there on the sidewalk?

_____

Chef Dale is cooking up some nutty nibbles. He made some for you, too! Add them to the scene. Then draw your own tasty treats!

Who doesn't love the rain? Draw a picture of what you like to do on rainy days!

Answer the questions to solve the crossword puzzle.

Across

3: What color is my dress?

5: What color is my hat?

Down

1: What color is my hat?

2: What color are my shoes?

3: What color is my dress?

4: What color is my hat?

Love is in the air! What did Mickey do
to earn a kiss from Minnie? Draw
it in the thought bubble.

Goofy loves to go snorkeling! Draw in what he sees underwater.

Blooop
Blooop
Blooop

This picture of Mickey and Pluto is all mixed up. Label the correct spot for each piece.

What's Donald so angry about? Draw a picture of it. Now draw something that would make Donald happy again.

Bambi has lots of pals in the forest. Draw them!

Minnie and Daisy are planning a special surprise for Mickey and Donald.

But a special surprise needs a special outfit!

Next it's off to the store. Minnie and Daisy have to get some supplies!

The Party and More Store

At home, Minnie hangs
balloons everywhere.

Daisy's busy in the kitchen making a special treat.

Finally everything's ready.
Minnie and Daisy set the table.

Mickey and Donald knock on the door and come inside.

"Surprise!" Minnie and Daisy shout. What a great party!

Bambi and Thumper love to play hide-and-seek. Help each of them think of a good place to hide.

SuperMinnie has a super disguise! Give her some super friends to fight crime with!

Mickey and Donald are making snowmice and snowducks. Help them finish their creations! What would you look like as a snowman? Add it to the scene!

Goofy loves listening to music.
Make up your own song lyrics
for him to sing along to.

Snap! Mickey loves to take pictures.
Draw a picture of your favorite moment.

Whee! Minnie loves going to the water park. Give her some fun rides to go on!

Chip and Dale are getting ready for winter. Help them store nuts around the forest.

Daisy's name appears in the grid 15 times. Can you find all 15? They may run across, down, or backward. Cross her name off the list each time you find it in the grid.

1. DAISY   **6.** DAISY   **11.** DAISY

2. DAISY   **7.** DAISY   **12.** DAISY

3. DAISY   **8.** DAISY   **13.** DAISY

4. DAISY   **9.** DAISY   **14.** DAISY

5. DAISY   **10.** DAISY   **15.** DAISY

D	D	I	I	S	Y	Y	D	D
D	A	I	S	Y	S	D	A	A
A	A	S	I	D	I	S	I	D
I	S	D	I	D	A	I	S	Y
S	Y	S	I	A	D	A	Y	S
Y	S	D	S	I	I	A	S	S
S	D	A	I	S	Y	S	I	A
I	D	I	Y	Y	S	I	A	D
A	Y	S	I	A	D	D	D	Y
D	D	Y	S	I	A	D	D	Y

Time for school! Draw what Mickey, Donald, and Goofy are learning about on the board.

Which Flower isn't the same? Circle him. Draw your own Flower that's different from all the others.

Mickey and Pluto are playing fetch. Draw a stick for Pluto to chase after. What else could he bring back to Mickey?

Match the Cuties to their shadows by drawing lines between them.

a.

b.

c.

d.

e.

f.

g.

h.

i.

j.

k.

Donald is helping Daisy in her vegetable garden. What is she growing? What tools does she need to make her garden grow?

What is Minnie watching? Add it to the scene.

Mickey loves to listen to music. What are your favorite songs? Write the titles, then draw pictures to go with them!

Boom!!!
Boom!!
Boom!

Boom!!!
Boom!!
Boom!

_____

_____

_____

**Thumper sent Bambi a secret message.
Can you help him decode it?**

Pᶐmd Nmynu,

Yᶐᶐf yᶐ mf ftᶐ

bazp. U tmhᶐ m

egdbdueᶐ rad kag.

Xahᶐ,

Ftgybᶐd

D _ _ _ _ _ _ _ _,

_ _ _ _ _ _ _ _ _ _ _ _

_ _ _ _ _ _ _ _ _

_ _ _ _ _ _ _ _ _ _ _

_ _ _ _,

_ _ _ _ _ _

MNOPQR S TUVWXYZABCDEFGHI JKL
ABCDEF GHI JKLMNOPQRS TUVWXYZ

Donald wants to pick the perfect pumpkin for Daisy. Help him out by giving him more pumpkins to choose from.

Mickey and Goofy are camping out.
Give them sleeping bags and a big
campfire to keep them warm.

SuperChip has lost his cape! Give him a new one. What else does he need to fight crime?

Minnie and Daisy are getting dessert at the sweets shop. Help them narrow down their choices by solving these problems. Then draw your favorite candy on the empty shelf.

 = 9

= 6

= 7

= ____

= ____

= ____

It's nighttime in the forest and everyone's getting ready for bed. Draw the moon and the stars. Then give Bambi someone to cuddle up with.

Splash! Jumping in puddles is so much fun! Give Mickey some friends to spend his rainy day with.

Fill in the rest of Pluto's story with your own drawings

1. Oh, no! Pluto lost his bone! Where could it be?

2. Is it buried under the tree?

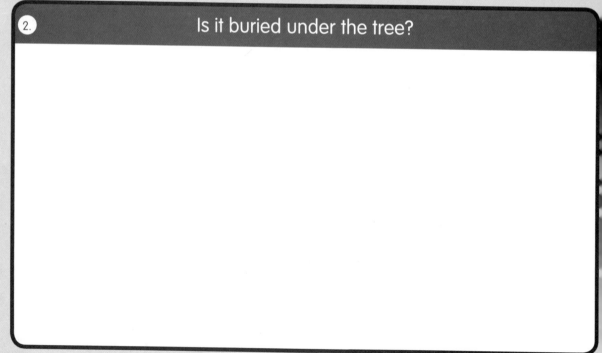

3. Did he leave it in his doghouse?

4. Congratulations, Pluto. You found it!

SuperCuties to the rescue! Connect the dots on each page to help SuperMinnie and SuperMickey save the day.

Start
1

End

Chip and Dale are having a snowball fight!
Give them each a pile of snowballs to throw!
What else can they do with the snow?

Donald and Mickey want to find the perfect presents for Daisy and Minnie. Help them narrow it down by solving these problems.

Donald holding  $-$ $= 3$

Mickey holding  $-$ $= 4$

Donald holding  − = _____

Mickey holding − = _____

Daisy and Minnie are redecorating Minnie's room. Add your own touch to their design.

Find the picture that only appears once and circle it.

There are six differences in these two scenes. Can you find them all?

ZZZZ . . . Nap time for Mickey and Minnie. Draw more branches on the tree to keep the sun from waking them. What else can you draw in the sky?

ZZZZZZZ . . .

Zzzzzzz . . .

Take a bow! Daisy is acting in a play. Give her an audience to cheer her on. What else would be onstage?

Mickey, Donald, and Goofy are running a race. Draw a track for them. Be sure to include the finish line!

Write the name of each character below.
Then find their names in the word search.
They may run across or down.

_____

_____

_____

_____

```
G  F  M  I  C  K  E  Y
A  L  I  Z  P  R  Q  R
M  B  N  L  P  U  G  X
D  O  N  A  L  D  O  A
I  D  I  P  U  A  O  F
H  N  E  O  T  M  F  L
V  B  R  S  O  S  Y  C
G  M  T  E  U  Q  J  K
```

Something's not right in this scene. Can you find five things that are out of place?

Daisy and Minnie love finding shapes in the clouds. What do you see in the clouds? Draw some more fun figures for them to look at.

Mickey and Goofy are spending the day with Donald, but they can't reach him! Help them find their way through the maze.

Draw yourself as a Disney Cutie!